HEMI'S PET

Houghton Mifflin Company
Boston 1987

A Dorothy Butler Book

Published in the United States by Houghton Mifflin Company
Originally published in New Zealand in 1985
by Reed Methuen Publishers Ltd, 39 Rawene Road, Auckland 10

ISBN: 0-395-43665-6

Printed in Hong Kong

10 9 8 7 6 5 4 3 2 1

HEMI'S PET

by Joan de Hamel / Illustrated by Christine Ross

Rata was only three, but she often
went to school. Her big
brother, Hemi, who was seven,
went to school every day.

When Rata went along to visit him,
the teacher often let her stay
and play for a while.

Soon, the school was going to have
a pet show. All the children
in the class had a pet of some
sort, except Hemi.

He was sad not to have a pet
to show.
Rata asked, "What is a pet?"

Hemi said, "A pet is
something that's alive and you
love it and look after it."
Rata asked, "Am I your pet?"

Hemi began to smile and smile.

The day of the pet show
he washed Rata's hands. He
brushed her hair. He dressed her
in her favorite dress.

Mother said, "Look at Rata!"
Dad said, "Where are you off to, love?"

"I'm taking her to school," said Hemi.
"I'm looking after her today."

At school Hemi told everyone,
"Look! I've got a pet, too! A pet sister."
The other children laughed and
said, "Don't be so dumb. A sister
isn't a pet!"

Hemi shouted, "She is so! She's alive and I love her and look after her, so she's my pet."

The children said, "But she doesn't have four legs like a pet."

Hemi said, "Neither does that bird."

The children said, "But she doesn't have feathers like a bird."

Hemi said, "Neither does that cat."

The children said, "But she doesn't have fur like a cat."

And Hemi said, "Neither does that fish."

The children said, "But she doesn't have a tail like a fish."

And Hemi said, "Neither does that guinea pig."

So they let him enter Rata as a pet sister. Hemi and Rata won the prize for the most original pet.

The prize was a red ribbon and a
bag of potato chips. They ate the chips.

But Hemi tied the red ribbon in Rata's hair and told her she could keep it forever and ever.